The Halloween Cat

by Christine Ricci
illustrated by Zina Saunders

Ready-to-Read

Simon Spotlight/Nick Jr.

New York   London   Toronto   Sydney

visit us at www.abdopublishing.com

Reinforced library bound edition published in 2009 by Spotlight, a division of ABDO Publishing Group, 8000 West 78th Street, Edina, Minnesota 55439. Published by agreement with Simon Spotlight, an imprint of Simon & Schuster Children's Publishing Division.

SIMON SPOTLIGHT

An imprint of Simon & Schuster Children's Publishing Division
1230 Avenue of the Americas, New York, NY 10020

Library of Congress Cataloging-in-Publication Data

This title was previously cataloged with the following information:

Ricci, Christine.
  The Halloween cat / by Christine Ricci ; illustrated by Zina Saunders.
  p. cm. -- (Ready-to-read. Level 1; #6)
  "Based on the TV series Dora the Explorer as seen on Nick Jr."
Summary: Dora and Boots help a small black cat find its way home to the Candy Castle on Halloween. Features rebuses.
  1. Rebuses. [1. Halloween--Fiction. 2. Cats--Fiction. 3. Rebuses.] I. Saunders, Zina, ill. II. Dora the explorer (Television program) III. Title. IV. Ready-to-read. Level 1, Dora the explorer.
PZ7.R355 Hal 2004
[E]--dc22   2003018335

ISBN-13: 978-1-59961-439-7 (reinforced library bound edition)
ISBN-10: 1-59961-439-1 (reinforced library bound edition)

All Spotlight books have reinforced library binding
and are manufactured in the United States of America.

Hi, I am  .

DORA

I am dressed as a

DINOSAUR

for Halloween.

 is dressed as a !

BOOTS   BANANA

We see a small 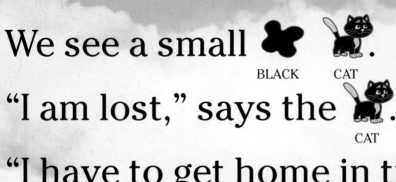 .

BLACK CAT

"I am lost," says the 🐱 .

CAT

"I have to get home in time

for the big Halloween

party!"

and I will help

the .

Will you help

too?

The 🗺 (MAP) knows where the 🐱 (CAT) lives. "The 🐱 (CAT) lives in the 🏰 (CANDY CASTLE) with the 🧙 (GOOD WITCH)," says 🗺 (MAP).

We have to go to the  HAUNTED HOUSE

and into the to get to

SPOOKY FOREST

the .

CANDY CASTLE

We are at the  .

HAUNTED HOUSE

It is dark inside!

We need something to

help us see in the dark.

Can you spot the ?

FLASHLIGHT

There are many  DOORS

in the HAUNTED HOUSE .

A  says, "Find the
GHOST   DOOR

with 7 🕷🕷."
SEVEN   SPIDERS

Yay! We made it out of
the .

HAUNTED HOUSE

Now we will go to the  .

SPOOKY FOREST

Do you see the ?

SPOOKY FOREST

Uh-oh, here is a  .

GATE

 says an

MAP ORANGE KEY

will open the .

GATE

Do you see an 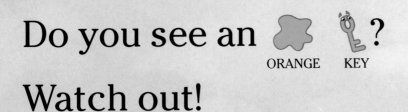 ?

ORANGE   KEY

Watch out!

 will try to swipe the 🔑 .

SWIPER   KEY

Say " 🦊 , no swiping!"

SWIPER

Yay! We stopped  .

And we opened the !

SWIPER

GATE

" says the

MAP   RED   LEAVES

will lead us out of the

. "

SPOOKY FOREST

We made it out of the 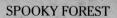 !

SPOOKY FOREST

Now we have to find .

CANDY CASTLE

Here we are at  .
CANDY CASTLE

But how do we get in?

"Use the 🧹 !" says
BROOMSTICK

the 🐈 .
CAT

Wow! We are flying!

Hello,  !

GOOD WITCH

We did it! The  is home
CAT

with the  .
GOOD WITCH

Happy Halloween!